SILENT ECHOES

NAMOOS NAVEED

Made with ♥ on the Notion Press Platform
www.notionpress.com

To the girls who carry their silence like a wound,

who have been unheard, unseen, unbelieved.

To those who have fought battles within themselves,

who have stitched their own hearts back together

with nothing but quite strength and borrowed hope.

And to every woman who has ever been told

she is less because of what has been taken from her--

you are not ruined, you are not unworthy.

you are a whole, even in your breaking.

This story is for you.

Contents

Foreword

This is not just a story. It is voice-- one that has long been buried beneath silence, shame, and the weight of past no one wanted to hear. It is the voice of a girl who was never given a space to greive, to rage, to exist as she was, without judgement.

Zara's journey is not about survival alone--it is about reclaiming what was stolen, about finding light in the darkest corners of memory , about healing in a world that refuses to see her wounds. She is not just one girl; she is many. Her pain is echoed in countless hearts, in whispers shared behind closed doors, in eyes that have long stopped hoping for justice.

This story does not seek to offer easy answers. It does not promise redemption in the way the world defines it. Instead it follows the quite, difficult path of a girl who learns to make peace with her ghosts--not by erasing them, but by learning to live with them.

To every reader who finds a reflection of themselves in Zara's pain, this book is for you. May you find strength in her journey, and may it remind you that even in silence, you are not alone.

Preface

Stories of pain are often left untold, buried under the weight of shame, disbelief and fear. This story is one of those--one that could have remained hidden, like many others. But silence has never healed wounds. This book is not about vengence or seeking validation. It is about a girl, Zara, who was forced to carry a burden too heavy for her young shoulders. It is about the wounds that never stopped aching. It is about the absence of justice, the betrayal of those who were meant to protect her, and the struggle to find meaning in a world that dismissed her suffering. Yet, at its core, this story is not just about pain. It is about resillience. About a girl who learns that healing is not forgetting, that love does not always come in the form we expect, and that survival is sometimes the greatest rebellion. The journey within these pages is raw, unfiltered and deeply personal. It does not follow the arc of traditional redemption. Instead, it mirrors the truth of so many lives--where closure is a myth, justice is elusive but the strength to go on remains.

This book is for those who have known the kind of silence that screams.

For those who have waited to be heard. For those who are still finding their way through the darkness.

Zara's story belongs to many, but most of all, it belongs to her.

and, now, it belongs to you.

Acknowledgements

This story would have not been possible without the voices--both spoken and unspoken--that have shaped it.

To the women whose pain has been dismissed, whose truths have been doubted, and those whose strength has gone unrecognised--you are the reason this story exists. Your silent resilliance, your unseen battles, and your quite survival have given this story its breath.

To those who have suffered in silence, yet continued to rise every day--you are not forgotten. This book is a testament to your courage.

To the ones who listen, who believe, who stand beside the wounded without asking them to prove their pain--thank you. The world needs more of you.

And finally, to every reader who carries their own wounds, who finds a part of themselves in Zara's journey--this story is yours now. May it remind you that you are not alone.

Prologue

There are wounds that time does not touch. Wounds that exist beneath the skin, burried so deep they become part of the body's rhythm--woven into breath, threaded through memory.

Zara has lived with such wounds. She has carried them in silence, in the spaces between words, in the emptiness of nights that refuse to forget. She has learned to walk with them, to hide them beneath the weight of normalcy, to convince, to covince the world--and herself--that she is whole.

But silence is never empty. It is filled with echoes, with ghosts that refuse to rest.

Tonight, in the city that has always held her secrets, the past begins to stir. It comes not as a sudden storm, but as a whisper, a shadow at the edge of her mind. The streets of Srinagar breathe with memories, and in their stillness, something inside her shifts.

She does not know it yet, but this is the beginning. The unraveling. The moment before the silence finally breaks.

1

The Weight Of Silence

The call to Fajr echoed through the misty streets of Srinagar, piercing the stillness of dawn. Zara sat by the small wooden window of her family's ancestral home, her breath clouding the frosty glass as she traced invisible patterns with her finger. The low hum of the muezzin's voice stirred an ache within her—a hollow, familiar grief she couldn't escape.

She had always loved this hour of the day, where the world was neither fully awake nor entirely asleep, as though time itself hesitated to move forward. It was here, in this fragile stillness, that her mind broke free of the carefully constructed walls she'd built. It was here that the past crept in, unbidden and unforgiving.

The scent of burning firewood drifted in from the neighbor's home, mingling with the crisp winter air, but it brought no comfort. Zara closed her eyes, letting the memories seep in like the cold, suffocating and relentless.

She was eight years old again. The room was dimly lit by single bulb that flickered like a dying heartbeat. She remembered the roughness of the floor against her small hands, the muffled sound of laughter from the adults in the next room. And him—his shadow looming over her like a thundercloud. Her chest tightened, her fingers curling a into fists. She could still hear his voice, sickly sweet, whispering words she didn't understand at the time. But she understood now, and the understanding was a wound that refused to heal.

Her eyes snapped open, the memory dissipating like smoke, but the heaviness lingered. Zara pressed her forehead to the cold glass, her breath uneven. "Ya Allah," she whispered, her voice barely audible. "Why do I still feel him here, in my skin, in my bones?"

Her faith had once been a refuge, but now it felt distant, like the snow-capped peaks that surrounded her city—majestic but unreachable. Every prayer felt hollow, every plea unanswered. She wanted to scream, to claw her way out of this prison of her own mind, but all she could do was sit there, a silent witness to her own unraveling.

The sound of footsteps on the creaky wooden floor behind her startled her. Zara turned to see her younger brother, Azaan, rubbing sleep from his eyes. He gave her a curious look but said nothing, padding away toward the kitchen.

For a moment, she envied him—his innocence, his ignorance of the shadows that lurked in the corners of their world. But envy quickly gave way to guilt. She couldn't protect herself back then. How could she ever protect him?

Zara straightened up, wiping her face with trembling hands. She had survived another night. The dawn had come, as it always did, indifferent to her suffering. But a part of her clung to the hope that maybe, just maybe, this day would be different.

2

Fractures Beneath the Surface

The morning light slowly seeped into the room, casting long shadows on the worn wooden floor. Zara had not moved since her brother's footsteps faded away, her eyes unfocused, staring into the distance. The faint echo of the muezzin's voice still lingered in her ears, an incessant reminder of a time when faith had been a refuge, not a battlefield.

She pulled her shawl tighter around her shoulders, feeling the weight of her own skin, the way it seemed to cling to her, a constant reminder of everything she wanted to forget. Her hands, delicate but strong, trembled as they reached for the Quran on the low wooden shelf beside her. She opened it, fingers brushing the pages as though searching for something—anything—that could bring the peace she so desperately needed.

The words were familiar, comforting even, but they felt distant, like an old friend who had become a stranger. Bismillah, she whispered to herself, and for a moment, the tension in her chest eased, but only briefly. The weight returned, heavier than before. Zara's eyes wandered to the small family photograph on the wall—the one of her mother, her father, and herself, taken years ago when life had still seemed whole.

She could almost hear her mother's voice, soft and soothing, calling her name. Zara, she would say, the name like a prayer itself. But the memory was fading, slipping through her fingers like grains of sand.

The sound of Azaan's laughter broke her reverie. He was outside, playing with his friends in the yard, their voices carrying through the thin walls of the house. Zara's heart clenched at the sound—innocence, freedom, things she couldn't afford. She hadn't felt lightness in years.

A knock on the door startled her. She turned sharply, her heartbeat quickening.

"Zara?" It was her father's voice, hesitant and soft.

She stood quickly, wiping her face as though she could erase the traces of the storm that had raged inside her. The door creaked open, and her father stepped in. His eyes were tired, the lines on his face deepening with the weight of years lived in silence.

"Is everything alright?" His voice was gentle, but there was an unspoken worry that lingered between them. Zara forced a smile, one that didn't quite reach her eyes.

"I'm fine, Baba. Just... thinking," she replied, her voice betraying the calm she tried to project.

Her father nodded slowly, but his gaze lingered, searching for the truth in her eyes. It was a look Zara had known all her life, the one that asked if she was still the daughter he used to know, or if the girl who had once been full of laughter and hope had been lost to the silence.

"I know it's hard," he said softly, stepping closer. "The world is different now. But you don't have to carry it all alone, Zara. We're here for you."

Her throat tightened. We're here for you. The words were kind, but they felt like a promise Zara wasn't sure could be kept. She had learned long ago that some wounds didn't heal, and some battles were fought in silence, even if you had someone beside you.

"I know, Baba," she whispered, the words heavy in her mouth.

Her father sighed, his gaze dropping to the floor. "I never wanted this for you, Zara. You... you shouldn't have to bear so much."

Zara looked at him then, seeing the quiet anguish in his eyes. He had never spoken of it before, not in words that were this raw. He had always been her protector, her pillar, but in that moment, she realized that he, too, carried burdens too heavy to share.

The silence between them stretched, thick and suffocating. Zara opened her mouth to speak, but the words didn't come. She couldn't explain what it felt like to be haunted by something that no one else could see. She couldn't tell him how the past had carved its mark into her, how it made her doubt everything she had once believed in.

"I need to go," Zara said finally, her voice barely above a whisper.

Her father nodded, the understanding between them unspoken but deep. "Be careful."

As she left the room, the weight of her father's gaze lingered in the air, a reminder of all the things left unsaid. Zara stepped into the cold morning, the world outside as still and frozen as the silence in her heart.

3

The Echo of a Forgotten song

Zara stepped outside, the frigid air biting at her skin, and immediately the sounds of the city swarmed around her. The streets of Srinagar were never quiet, even in the early morning. Vendors called out to passersby, the rhythmic tapping of wooden carts on cobblestone, the soft murmur of conversations from nearby homes—life persisted, indifferent to the silence that choked Zara from within.

She drew her shawl tighter, her hands buried deep in its folds. It had been too long since she had truly left the house, too long since she had allowed herself to exist in the world beyond her grief. But today, there was a quiet urgency inside her, a pull that urged her forward even though she didn't know why.

She moved through the market, her eyes scanning the familiar faces. The same vendors, the same children darting between the stalls, laughing and shouting, oblivious to the weight that hung like a fog over the city. It was as if the world carried on without her, as if she were just another ghost in the crowd, drifting through life without a true purpose.

As she walked past a small shop selling spices and woven carpets, the familiar scent of saffron and cardamom hit her with unexpected force. She stopped, her breath catching in her throat. The smell was like a portal, transporting her back to simpler times, back to when her mother would knead dough for roti in the kitchen, her laughter filling the air like the sound of a song.

Ya Allah, not now, Zara thought, her chest tightening as the memory threatened to consume her. She closed her eyes briefly, as if trying to erase the ache that had taken root deep inside her. But the memories were persistent, clinging to her like shadows.

"Zara?"

The voice broke through her reverie, and she turned sharply, her heart skipping a beat. It was Amir.

Her breath hitched. She hadn't seen him in years, not since the last time their paths had crossed under circumstances neither of them cared to revisit. Amir, with his quiet charm and his sharp, calculating eyes. The boy she had once known, but who felt like a stranger now.

He stood there, a few feet away, his expression unreadable. The faintest hint of a smile tugged at the corner of his lips, but it didn't reach his eyes. Zara felt her pulse quicken, the past and present colliding in that single moment.

"What are you doing here?" she asked, her voice sounding more distant than she intended.

Amir shifted his weight, his hands shoved into his coat pockets. "I could ask you the same thing. Last I heard, you'd disappeared into the quiet of your family's house, like the rest of the world didn't exist."

Zara forced herself to meet his gaze, her stomach twisting. "I'm just... living," she replied, though the words felt hollow.

Amir studied her for a moment, his eyes softening. "You don't have to pretend, you know. Not with me." He hesitated, as if weighing his next words. "I know what you've been through, Zara. I—"

She held up a hand, cutting him off before he could finish. "Don't."

It was the same with Amir. Words were always too much, too heavy. He had known parts of her, parts of her pain, but he hadn't known the full story. No one had.

"Zara, I—" Amir began again, but Zara took a step back, her chest tightening as her heart thudded painfully against her ribcage. She couldn't do this, couldn't let him probe the wounds she had buried so deep.

"I need to go," she said abruptly, turning away before he could say anything else. She felt his gaze on her back, but she didn't stop. She couldn't stop.

As she walked away, her mind raced, the weight of his words pressing down on her. I know what you've been through. Did he really? Did anyone?

But more than that, a question gnawed at her. Why had he come back now? And what did he want from her? She had buried that part of her life, hidden it in the deepest corners of her heart. It was supposed to stay there, untouched. But Amir had pulled it out, whether he meant to or not.

And as the cold air wrapped around her, Zara felt something shift inside her. Maybe it wasn't the world that had abandoned her. Maybe it was herself.

4

The Weight of Remembering

Zara hurried down the narrow alleyway, her footsteps quick and uneven. The air, crisp and biting, seemed to reflect the sudden rush in her chest. Amir's presence had unsettled her more than she cared to admit. She could still feel the weight of his gaze on her, as if he had opened a door she wasn't ready to walk through.

The city around her was unchanged—Srinagar's streets bustling with the usual hum of life. Vendors shouted from their stalls, children ran through the market, and the distant call of the muezzin echoed across the rooftops. But it all felt muted, distant, as if Zara were caught in a haze, her senses overwhelmed by the memories Amir had dragged back to the surface.

She didn't want to think about him—not now. Not after everything that had happened. But it was impossible to escape. His words echoed in her mind, a constant refrain: I know what you've been through.

Did he? Did anyone?

Zara found herself on the edge of Dal Lake, the cold water stretching out before her like a mirror, reflecting the mountains that surrounded the city. She stood there, staring into the vast emptiness, hoping the stillness would quiet the storm within her. But the silence only amplified the weight of her thoughts.

What does he want from me? she wondered. After all these years, why had Amir resurfaced in her life? Was it pity? Guilt? Or was there something more—something she wasn't ready to face?

She closed her eyes, taking a slow, shaky breath. The memories came rushing back, unbidden, unstoppable.

She was sixteen again, sitting in Amir's family home. It was a small house, warm and cozy, filled with the scent of cooking and the sound of quiet conversations. She remembered the way Amir's laughter had filled the room, how easy it had been to talk to him, to be with him.

Back then, he had been the one person who made her forget. The one person who made her feel like the past didn't matter.

But the past always catches up. It always returns.

Zara's eyes snapped open. The memories faded, but the ache remained. The ache of being seen, truly seen, by someone she had once trusted, someone she had once let in. Amir had known her before the walls had gone up, before the darkness had swallowed her. And that knowledge—what did it mean now?

I'm not that girl anymore, she told herself. I can't be her again.

But what if the person she had become wasn't enough?

A sharp voice broke through her thoughts. "Zara?"

She turned quickly, her heart hammering in her chest. It was her father, standing a few feet away, his expression a mix of concern and resignation.

"You've been out here for hours," he said quietly, his voice soft but edged with worry. "Is everything alright?"

Zara nodded, though the answer was far from true. She couldn't bring herself to speak about the turmoil she was feeling, not to him. He had enough to carry.

"I'm fine, Baba," she said, the words falling from her lips like a familiar lie. She hadn't meant to come out here, hadn't meant to disappear into the quiet of the lake. But there was something in the vastness of the water that made her feel small, insignificant—like a part of her that had been lost was somehow drifting back to the surface.

Her father didn't look convinced. He took a step closer, his eyes searching hers. "Zara, you don't have to carry it alone, you know."

The weight of his words settled in her chest like a stone. She wanted to tell him, to share the burden, but the words were trapped inside her. How could she explain the war raging within her? How could she tell him that she was fighting not just the world around her, but the ghosts of her past?

"I know," Zara whispered, her voice barely audible.

Her father sighed deeply, his gaze shifting to the lake. "You remind me of your mother," he said softly. "She used to sit by the water for hours, thinking. I always wondered what went through her mind. I never asked. I think I was afraid to know."

Zara's heart tightened. She could see her mother in his words, in the way his voice cracked just slightly. Her mother had always been the strong one, the calm presence in their home. But now, even her father was broken—carrying a weight that had slowly bent him, like a tree caught in a storm.

"I miss her," Zara said, her voice raw with emotion.

Her father nodded, his eyes distant. "I know, habibti. I miss her too."

For a long moment, neither of them spoke. The only sound was the soft rustle of the leaves in the trees, the distant murmur of the city behind them. Zara felt the weight of her father's presence, the silent understanding between them. They were both holding onto pieces of the past, pieces that didn't seem to fit together anymore.

"I need to go," Zara said suddenly, breaking the stillness. Her father gave her a long, searching look but said nothing. She turned and walked away from him, back towards the crowded streets, the noise, the life. But inside, the quiet remained.

5

The Unspoken Things Between Us

Zara woke up to the sound of Azaan's laughter, a soft, innocent sound that filled the house with life. For a moment, it felt like nothing had changed. The world outside was still frozen in winter, the mornings cold and quiet, and the bustle of the city a distant hum. Yet inside her, everything felt different.

Her mind kept returning to Amir, his face etched into the back of her eyelids, his voice still hanging in the air. He had reappeared, and with him, everything she had buried—the memories, the guilt, the pain—had risen to the surface once again. She had hoped time would smooth over the rough edges of the past, but it hadn't. If anything, the weight had only grown heavier, pressing against her chest like a physical presence.

She didn't want to face him. Not yet.

But she knew it was inevitable. Her father had already spoken of him more than once—had even mentioned inviting him over for dinner. Zara's stomach churned at the thought. Dinner? As if nothing had happened. As if all those years of silence, of broken trust, could be erased by a few polite words over a plate of food.

Zara had always known her father wanted to hold onto the past, to hold onto old connections, to make things right in ways that felt impossible. But how could she? How could she make peace with someone who had been part of a life that had betrayed her?

As she sat in the kitchen, watching Azaan sip his tea, her thoughts drifted back to Amir. He was no longer the young man she had once known—he was something different now, someone who had lived through the same years of silence that she had. Yet, in his eyes, there was something Zara couldn't place. Was it guilt? Regret? Or something else entirely?

Zara's heart thudded painfully in her chest. She needed to confront this. She needed to know what Amir wanted, why he had come back. But more than that, she needed to understand what it meant for her—for the person she had become.

"Zara?" Azaan's voice broke through her thoughts. She turned to him, her little brother's eyes wide with curiosity.

"Are you okay?" he asked softly, sensing the tension in the air.

Zara forced a smile, reaching out to ruffle his hair. "I'm fine, Azaan. Just thinking."

Azaan looked at her for a long moment, his gaze sharp despite his youth. "You've been thinking about him, haven't you?"

Zara's breath caught in her throat. She didn't know what to say. Could he already sense it? How much of their shared past had seeped into his awareness? Had her own pain been that obvious to him?

"I don't want you to be sad," Azaan said quietly, his small hands fidgeting with the edge of his cup. "You're always the strong one, Zara."

Zara's heart clenched. He was right. She had always been the strong one—had always shielded him from the things she couldn't protect herself from. But now, in this moment, she felt anything but strong. She felt fragile, as if the weight of the past would break her if she didn't let it go.

"I'm not sad," she lied. "I'm just... thinking about everything that's happened."

Azaan nodded slowly, as if understanding far more than his years should allow. He stood up and walked over to her, placing his small hand on hers. "You don't have to carry it alone, you know," he said, his voice full of quiet certainty.

For a brief moment, Zara felt the sting of tears in her eyes, but she blinked them away. Azaan was right. She didn't have to carry it alone. But she didn't know how to share the burden. She didn't know if anyone could understand the weight of it all.

Later that evening, Zara found herself standing in the living room, her back to the door, her fingers nervously twirling the hem of her sleeve. The familiar sound of footsteps echoed through the house, and her heart skipped a beat. Amir had arrived.

Zara didn't turn around as she heard her father's voice greeting Amir with warmth, the sound of their conversation distant and muffled. She stood frozen, her mind racing. What would he say? What would she say?

The silence stretched on until finally, the sound of Amir's footsteps grew closer. Slowly, she turned around, her eyes locking with his. For a moment, neither of them spoke, the weight of years of separation hanging between them like an unspoken question.

Amir's eyes softened as they met hers. He looked older—more worn—but the familiarity of him was still there, like a ghost lingering in the room.

"Zara," he said, his voice a mix of hesitation and something else she couldn't quite place.

Zara didn't know what to feel. Anger? Relief? Confusion?

"I didn't think I'd see you again," Zara finally managed to say, her voice barely above a whisper. Her heart raced, and she fought to keep her emotions in check.

Amir took a step closer, his gaze steady. "I never wanted to hurt you, Zara," he said, his words carrying more weight than she expected. "But I know I did. I know I can never take that back."

Zara's chest tightened. She wanted to ask him everything—to demand answers, to confront the past. But something held her back. Could she truly handle the truth? Could she hear what he had to say after all these years?

Instead, she stood there in silence, feeling the years of grief and resentment settle in her chest, unwilling to let go.

"I just need to know why," Zara said finally, her voice raw. "Why now? Why after all this time?"

Amir's eyes darkened, and he exhaled sharply. "Because I need to make things right, Zara. For both of us."

Zara swallowed hard, the pain of his words cutting deeper than she had anticipated. Make things right? How could anything be made right after everything that had been lost?

Zara's hands trembled slightly as Amir's words hung in the air. He needed to make things right. The simplicity of that statement felt like an insult, like a cruel mockery of everything she had gone through.

She swallowed hard, the lump in her throat growing. How could he think that a few words, a return to the past, could somehow undo the years of pain? How could he expect her to just forgive him, to let him back into the space she had so carefully fortified?

"You can't make things right," Zara said, her voice low but firm. "Not after everything."

Amir flinched, his expression tightening. For a brief moment, his gaze flickered with guilt, and Zara saw the man he had become—not the carefree boy she had known, but someone who had lived through his own storms. It was as if the years between them had hollowed him out, leaving behind only regret and an attempt at redemption.

"I know that," Amir replied quietly. "I'm not asking for forgiveness, Zara. I don't expect that. I just... I needed to see you. I needed to know that you were still alive in there." He gestured toward her, as if encompassing the distance between them, the years of silence.

Zara felt the sting of his words, the subtle implication that she had become a stranger to him, someone locked behind walls so high no one could climb them. And yet, somewhere deep inside, the softest part of her ached at the truth. She had been hiding, hiding from him, from her past, from the world.

"I've been surviving, Amir," she said, the words bursting out of her before she could stop them. "That's all I've been doing. Surviving."

A silence followed, thick and suffocating. Amir's eyes softened, as though he wanted to say something more, something that could ease the ache between them. But he didn't. Instead, he stood there, waiting for her to speak again.

Zara took a step back, suddenly overwhelmed by the proximity. His presence, once comforting, now felt like a pressure, an invisible hand tightening around her chest. She wanted to tell him everything, wanted to scream at him for not being there when she needed him the most. But the words felt too large, too dangerous. And so, they remained lodged in her throat, unspoken.

"I don't know what you want from me," Zara said finally, her voice shaking. "I don't know how to make peace with this. How do I make peace with someone who—" Her words caught in her throat, the rest of the sentence dying before it could escape. She couldn't say it. Not yet.

Amir stepped forward, his face earnest, a quiet plea in his eyes. "Zara, I never meant for any of it to happen. But I... I wasn't there. I should have been. I should have protected you."

The rawness of his voice—filled with regret, remorse, and something deeper—touched a nerve within Zara. For a moment, she saw him as the person he had been when they were younger, the boy who had sworn to look out for her. But that boy was long gone. And in his place stood a man who had abandoned her when she needed him most.

"Maybe you should have," Zara said softly, her words full of quiet pain. "But you didn't."

Amir closed his eyes briefly, as though the weight of her words hit him like a blow. Then he nodded slowly, as if acknowledging the truth of what she had said.

"I can't change the past," Amir said, his voice now quieter, filled with a sense of resignation. "But I can't keep pretending that I'm not responsible for it, either."

Zara felt a tightness in her chest, a battle between wanting to forgive him and wanting to keep him away. It wasn't just about Amir anymore—it was about everything he represented: the brokenness of her past, the pain she had carried for so long, the weight of memory that never let her go.

For a long time, neither of them spoke. The air between them was thick with the unspoken things, with the ghosts of their shared history. Zara could hear the faint sound of Azaan's laughter from the other room, a reminder of innocence, of the life that had continued even after everything had fractured.

"I have to go," Zara said, her voice small, almost apologetic. "I can't do this right now, Amir. I need time."

Amir didn't argue. He didn't say anything to try to keep her there. Instead, he just nodded, his expression unreadable.

"I understand," he said quietly. "I'll give you space. But I won't give up. Not on you. Not on us."

Zara's heart clenched at his words, but she didn't have the strength to respond. She simply turned and walked away, the sound of her footsteps echoing in the silence of the house.

Outside, the cold air hit her like a slap to the face, but it did little to cool the fire burning inside her. Zara found herself standing by the old stone wall that surrounded her family's property, her hands gripping the cold stone as she tried to steady her breath.

Amir's words lingered in her mind. I won't give up. The promise felt both like a balm and a threat. Could she ever truly let him in again? Could she face what he represented—what he might uncover—without losing herself in the process?

The wind howled through the trees, and for a moment, Zara felt like she was caught between two worlds—the past she had left behind and the future she wasn't ready to face.

The weight of everything pressed down on her, a constant reminder that the more she tried to escape, the more tightly the past held onto her.

6

The Space Between Us

Zara retreated to her room, the door clicking shut behind her with a finality that echoed through the still house. The world outside had begun to darken, the soft light of dusk creeping into the room. She leaned against the cool windowpane, staring out at the snowy landscape that had always felt so constant, so familiar.

But nothing felt familiar anymore.

The conversation with Amir had shaken her more than she cared to admit. His presence, his words, had dug up everything she had tried to bury—everything she had learned to live without. She had always prided herself on being able to withstand the weight of her past, but Amir's return made that seem like a lie. How could she carry it all? How could she keep moving forward with these ghosts at her side?

The sound of footsteps outside her door pulled her from her thoughts. A soft knock followed.

"Zara?" It was her father's voice, low and cautious. She didn't respond at first, unsure of what to say. But after a moment, she opened the door.

Her father stood in the hallway, his posture tense. He looked older now, the weight of his own years and regrets weighing on him. There was a softness in his eyes, a kind of vulnerability she wasn't used to seeing.

"May I come in?" he asked, his voice gentle.

Zara stepped aside, and her father entered, closing the door behind him. For a long moment, neither of them spoke. The air between them was thick with unspoken words, and Zara felt the distance that had always been there between them widen, stretching like a chasm neither of them knew how to cross.

Finally, her father sat down on the edge of her bed, his hands resting in his lap.

"I know you're angry," he said quietly. "And I know you don't want to see him. But you need to understand..."

Zara cut him off, her voice sharper than she intended. "Understand what? That he's back, after all these years, pretending like nothing happened? Like the years of silence meant nothing?"

Her father looked at her, his eyes filled with a sadness she couldn't quite place. "Zara, he was part of our family. You know that."

Zara's breath caught in her throat. "I know what he was, but that doesn't change what happened. You don't get to just erase the past, Baba."

There was a long pause, and for a moment, Zara thought her father might leave. But instead, he let out a long sigh, running a hand through his graying hair.

"I never wanted you to go through what you did," he said, his voice thick with emotion. "I couldn't protect you, Zara. I failed you."

Zara felt something shift within her. The anger she had held onto for so long began to loosen, replaced by something raw and painful. "I never asked you to protect me, Baba," she whispered. "I just... I wanted you to see me. To see the hurt."

Her father's eyes softened, and he reached out, taking her hand in his. "I know. I know, and I'm sorry. I've always been afraid to face it. To face what happened to you."

Zara closed her eyes, the weight of his words pressing down on her. She had carried so much alone—so many things her father had never been able to see. And now, with Amir's return, it felt like the walls around her were crumbling, the things she had buried rising to the surface once again.

"You don't have to forgive him, Zara," her father continued, his voice a quiet plea. "But you need to find peace. For yourself."

Zara pulled her hand away gently, standing up and walking toward the window. The city lights twinkled in the distance, their soft glow a stark contrast to the turmoil inside her.

"I don't know if I can find peace, Baba," she said, her voice distant. "Not with him here. Not with everything that's come back."

Her father didn't respond immediately, but when he did, his voice was steady, almost resigned. "Then, do it for yourself. Don't let him define your peace. You are not the past, Zara. You are who you choose to be."

Zara turned to face him, her heart heavy with the weight of his words. She knew he was right, but it was easier said than done. How could she move forward when everything inside her screamed to hold onto the past?

"I'll try," she said quietly, the words tasting foreign on her tongue. She wasn't sure if she believed them, but they were all she could offer.

Her father stood up, placing a gentle hand on her shoulder. "That's all anyone can ask for, my daughter. Just try."

Zara nodded, though the chasm between them remained, filled with years of unspoken pain. She didn't know if she could ever bridge that gap, but for now, she would try. For herself.

Later that evening, after her father had left her room, Zara found herself sitting in the small living room, staring at the quiet flames in the hearth. Azaan sat beside her, his small frame leaning against hers, his head resting on her shoulder. He had always been her constant, the one part of her world that felt safe.

"You're quiet tonight," Azaan said, his voice soft but full of concern.

Zara smiled faintly, brushing a strand of his hair back. "Just thinking," she replied, though her thoughts were far from clear.

"You know, you don't have to be strong all the time," Azaan continued, his words simple but profound. "You can be sad if you want to. You can be angry. You don't have to carry everything alone."

Zara's chest tightened as she looked at him. How could she explain to him the weight she had carried for so long? How could she tell him that sometimes, it felt like too much to bear?

"I know," she whispered, her voice barely audible. "But sometimes, it's easier to just... pretend. Pretend everything's okay."

Azaan looked up at her, his eyes wide and trusting. "You don't have to pretend with me, Zara."

For the first time in a long while, Zara felt the weight of her own emotions. She wasn't just a protector anymore;

she was a person, fragile and flawed, and that was okay.

"I'm sorry," Zara murmured, her voice thick with unspoken emotions. "I should have been more... open with you."

Azaan shook his head, his smile gentle. "It's okay. I know you're doing your best."

Zara pulled him closer, wrapping her arms around him as if holding onto him could keep her from falling apart. And for a moment, she allowed herself to simply be. To be with him, with her family, and to let go of the heavy weight she had carried for so long.

7

Echoes of the Past

The days following Amir's return were filled with an uneasy silence, the kind that lingers between words that are never spoken. Zara found herself caught in a delicate balance, between the desire to confront the ghosts of her past and the instinct to retreat from them, to bury them deeper within the recesses of her heart.

Amir's presence, though still distant, seemed to infect every corner of the house, even the very air they breathed. Her father, while cordial, was always watching, waiting for something Zara couldn't name—perhaps for her to forgive, or for something to shift between them. But Zara couldn't see a shift, not yet. Not with so much unresolved.

As the days wore on, Zara began to notice subtle changes around the house. Her father, who had always been a figure of quiet authority, seemed more withdrawn, as though he was silently wrestling with his own demons. She could see the flickers of old pain in his eyes whenever Amir's name was mentioned, the shadows of a past he'd long tried to bury.

One evening, as Zara sat in the small kitchen preparing dinner, her father entered, his footsteps slow, deliberate.

There was something in the air tonight—something that felt different, like the tension before a storm.

"Zara," he began, his voice low, almost hesitant, "I've been meaning to talk to you about Amir."

Zara didn't look up as she chopped vegetables, her movements mechanical. She wasn't sure what to say, or if she even wanted to engage in this conversation. Every mention of Amir felt like a weight, pressing down on her chest.

"Baba," she said quietly, her voice careful, "I don't know what you want me to say. I've told you everything already."

Her father sighed, his eyes distant as he leaned against the doorframe. "I know you're angry with him. But I think you're angry with me too. And I'm not sure how much longer I can carry this..."

Zara paused, the knife in her hand trembling ever so slightly. She hadn't expected him to say that. Her father, who had always been a man of few words, was opening up to her in a way she didn't know how to respond to.

"I'm angry because I didn't protect you, Zara," her father continued, his voice thick with emotion. "And now... now I feel like I'm losing you. Like I lost you years ago, when I chose to bury what happened, when I chose to let Amir go."

Zara swallowed hard, her heart aching at the rawness of his confession. The distance between them felt vast, filled with years of silence and unspoken pain. She had never known that her father felt this way. But even in the depth of his guilt, Zara couldn't help but feel a sharp bitterness rise within her.

"I don't know if I can forgive him, Baba," she whispered, the weight of her words heavier than she expected. "And I don't know if I can forgive you either."

Her father's face fell, the pain in his eyes more than she could bear. He opened his mouth to say something, but the words failed him. Instead, he simply nodded, his shoulders sagging under the weight of everything they had both carried.

"I understand," he said quietly. "I just... I wanted you to know that I'm trying, Zara. I'm trying to make things right."

Zara felt a pang of guilt. She knew he was trying, but it wasn't enough. Not yet. She wasn't ready to let go of the years of hurt, of betrayal.

She turned away, her hand gripping the edge of the counter. "I'm not ready," she said, her voice soft but firm. "I'm not ready to forgive anyone."

Her father didn't respond. Instead, he gave her space, walking out of the kitchen without another word. Zara stood there, her heart heavy with the weight of his words, and the weight of her own emotions. She had never wanted to hurt him, but it seemed like that was the only thing she could do right now—hurt the people closest to her, because they had already hurt her first.

Later that night, after dinner had passed in strained silence, Zara found herself standing by the window once again, looking out at the quiet, snow-covered world. The stars shone brightly above, distant and indifferent, as if mocking her pain. She could hear the faint sounds of her father and Azaan talking in the other room, their voices muffled, but it was Amir's face that lingered in her thoughts.

She had tried to push him out, to block him from her mind. But he kept coming back, like a tide that wouldn't recede. And now, with every day that passed, she found herself wondering if she could ever truly escape the past.

The sound of a knock on the door interrupted her thoughts, and before she could answer, Amir stepped in, his presence looming in the doorway.

"Zara," he said quietly, his voice uncertain. "Can we talk?"

Zara didn't move. She didn't know how to respond, didn't know what to say to him. Part of her wanted to shut the door in his face, to retreat into the safety of her own silence. But something in his expression stopped her. There was no anger, no bravado. Just... a quiet pleading, a man seeking something he couldn't find within himself.

"I don't think we have anything left to say," Zara said, her voice thick with emotion, though her heart raced in her chest.

Amir didn't flinch. Instead, he stepped inside, his eyes never leaving hers. "I know," he replied softly. "But I need you to know... I'm not asking for your forgiveness. I just want... to be in your life again. Even if just for a moment."

Zara's breath hitched. She felt the walls around her trembling, her resolve beginning to crack. Could she really allow him back in, even for a moment? Was she strong enough to face him, to face what they had been, and what they could never be again?

"I can't give you that," Zara said quietly, her voice barely above a whisper. "I can't give you what you want."

Amir nodded slowly, as though he had expected nothing more. For a long moment, they simply stood there, the distance between them as vast as the space that had always existed.

"I'm sorry," Amir said at last, his voice thick with regret. "I'll go. I just... I needed to hear you say it."

Zara's chest tightened as he turned to leave, but before he could reach the door, she spoke again, her voice raw with emotion.

"Amir... you were part of my life once. And I don't know how to make sense of that anymore. I don't know how to make sense of you."

Amir paused, his back still to her, but his shoulders slumped in defeat. "I understand."

With that, he left, the door closing behind him with a soft thud that reverberated in the silence of the room.

8

A Quiet Reckoning

The days grew colder as winter deepened, and the weight of silence in the house seemed to grow heavier with each passing day. Zara found herself moving through the motions—preparing meals, attending to the needs of her family, but always with a sense of detachment. It was as though she were walking through a dream, unable to wake up from the quiet ache that lingered within her.

She had always prided herself on her ability to keep control, to hold herself together, no matter what storms raged within. But now, as the days stretched on, she realized that control was slipping through her fingers, and she wasn't sure how much longer she could keep up the façade of strength.

Zara sat at the kitchen table one evening, the low hum of the heater the only sound breaking the stillness. Azaan had already gone to bed, and her father was in his study, lost in his own thoughts, as usual. Zara was alone with her thoughts once again—thoughts that seemed to swirl around her in a relentless tide, pulling her under.

The past few days had been a blur of half-hearted attempts at normalcy. Her father had tried, in his own quiet way, to reach out to her, to bridge the distance that had grown between them. But every conversation felt like a reminder of all that had been lost—of all the things they could never speak of. There was a part of Zara that wanted to tell him everything, to scream and cry and let him know the depth of her pain. But she couldn't. She wasn't ready to face it, not yet. And so, she remained silent.

Her thoughts turned to Amir, as they often did now. His face lingered in her mind, his eyes full of remorse, his voice still echoing in her ears. Every time she thought she had buried him deep enough, he would resurface, like a shadow that refused to leave.

She closed her eyes, resting her head on the table, letting the quiet wash over her. It was in these moments, when she was completely still, that the weight of her memories pressed down on her the hardest. It was as if the ghosts of the past were whispering to her, reminding her of everything she had tried to forget.

"Zara."

Her father's voice broke through the silence, and she straightened up, startled. He stood in the doorway, his expression soft, but his eyes searching, as though trying to understand her in a way that had always eluded him.

"I... I didn't mean to disturb you," he said, stepping into the kitchen. "But I've been thinking. Maybe it's time for us to talk. To really talk."

Zara looked at him, her heart pounding in her chest. She wasn't sure if she was ready for this. She wasn't sure if she could handle another conversation filled with words that didn't quite reach the truth, with apologies that didn't feel real.

"I don't know what you want me to say, Baba," she said quietly, her voice tight. "I don't know if I have anything left to give."

Her father's gaze softened, and he walked over to her, sitting down across from her at the table. For a long moment, neither of them spoke. It was as if they were both trying to find the right words, trying to bridge a chasm that had grown too wide to cross.

"I know I've failed you, Zara," her father said finally, his voice thick with regret. "I've failed you in ways I can never fix. But I need you to know something... I never wanted you to carry this alone. I never wanted you to be burdened by all of this."

Zara felt her chest tighten at his words. She wanted to believe him, to let go of the resentment that had been building inside her for so long. But the hurt was still too fresh, still too raw.

"You don't understand," Zara whispered, her voice breaking. "You didn't protect me, Baba. You weren't there when I needed you the most."

Her father flinched, and for the first time, Zara saw something in his eyes that she had never seen before—shame. It was as if her words had struck him deep, as though they had finally pierced through the armor he had built around himself for years.

"I know," he said quietly. "And I'm sorry. I wish I could take back the years I lost. I wish I could have done more, been more."

Zara felt the familiar bitterness rise in her throat, but she swallowed it down. "It's too late for that, Baba," she said, her voice steady, though the pain in her chest was almost unbearable. "It's too late for apologies."

Her father closed his eyes for a moment, as though collecting himself. "I understand," he said softly. "But you're still my daughter. I may not be able to fix everything, but I'll always be here for you, Zara. No matter what."

Zara didn't know how to respond. Part of her wanted to scream, to tell him how much he had failed her, to remind him of all the times she had been left to face the darkness alone. But another part of her, the part that still loved him, wanted to let go of the anger, to find some way to forgive him.

"I don't know if I can forgive you, Baba," she said, her voice barely above a whisper. "I don't know if I can forgive anyone."

Her father's gaze softened, and he reached across the table, taking her hand in his. "I don't expect you to forgive me right now. I don't expect anything from you. All I want is for you to know that I love you, and that I'm sorry."

Zara squeezed his hand, though she didn't know if she could truly believe him. But in that moment, she realized something—maybe forgiveness wasn't something that happened all at once. Maybe it was something that took time, something that couldn't be rushed. And maybe, just maybe, she could begin to let go of the past, one small piece at a time.

Later that night, as Zara lay in bed, she found herself staring at the ceiling, her mind swirling with thoughts of her father, of Amir, and of everything she had lost. She didn't have all the answers, and she didn't know if she ever would. But for the first time in a long while, she felt a small spark of hope. Maybe, just maybe, healing was possible.

And maybe, someday, she would be able to look at her father—and at herself—and say, "I forgive you."

9

The Weight of Forgiveness

The days blurred together, the sharp edge of winter beginning to soften as the first signs of spring appeared in the distant hills of Srinagar. But inside Zara, nothing seemed to change. The cold, the ache of her past, clung to her as tightly as ever. The house, though warmer with the onset of the new season, still felt like a place of confinement, each room echoing with the ghosts of memories too painful to confront.

Zara tried to move through each day with a sense of purpose—feeding her family, attending to the small rituals of home life—but there was a part of her that remained disconnected. It was as though she were watching herself from a distance, seeing the motions of her life without truly feeling them. She longed to feel alive again, to feel something other than the weight of sorrow and regret that seemed to hang over her like a dark cloud.

One evening, as she sat by the window, watching the sun dip below the horizon, Azaan came in from the yard, his hands covered in mud from playing outside. He was still young, still innocent to the world's harsh realities, and for a moment, Zara envied him. He had not yet learned the weight of betrayal, the cost of silence. He had not yet seen the cracks that marred the foundation of their family.

"Azaan," Zara said quietly, her voice softer than she intended. "Come here, let me clean your hands."

He looked at her, his face lighting up with a smile. "I'm fine, Zara. I like the mud."

Zara couldn't help but smile at his stubbornness. He reminded her so much of herself at that age—determined, full of life, unaware of the heavy things that waited in the wings. As she took his hands and began cleaning the dirt off, Azaan looked up at her, his expression thoughtful.

"Zara," he began, his voice unusually serious for a boy of his age. "Why don't you talk to Baba much anymore?"

The question took Zara by surprise. She stopped what she was doing, her fingers stilling on his hands. "What do you mean?"

"You and Baba don't talk like you used to," Azaan said, looking up at her with wide, searching eyes. "It's like something's different. Like you're angry."

Zara's heart clenched at his words. She had tried so hard to shield him from the tension, to keep him from sensing the rift between her and their father. But Azaan, in his simple honesty, had seen it all. He was more perceptive than she gave him credit for.

"I'm not angry, Azaan," Zara said softly, forcing a smile. "I'm just... tired. It's been a long time, and sometimes, we need space to figure things out."

Azaan studied her for a moment, as though trying to understand, before he nodded. "Okay," he said simply, and ran off to his room.

Zara watched him go, her chest heavy with guilt. She had always wanted to protect him from the pain she had endured, but it seemed that no matter how hard she tried, the cracks were beginning to show. Azaan had always been the light in her life, the one thing she had been able to hold onto, and yet, even he had begun to sense the darkness she carried.

The next few days passed in a haze. Zara went through the motions of daily life, but every conversation with her father felt strained, every encounter with Amir left her more unsettled than the last. The weight of what had happened between them—the things they had never spoken of—hung over her like a cloud she could not escape.

One afternoon, as she walked through the old streets of Srinagar, her thoughts consumed with the ache of it all, she found herself standing outside the mosque. The familiar call to prayer echoed through the streets, a sound that had once brought her peace, but now felt like a distant memory. Zara had not been to the mosque in weeks. Her faith, once a refuge, now seemed like a fragile thing, easily broken by the weight of her grief.

She stepped inside, the cool air of the mosque wrapping around her like a cloak. The quiet was a relief, but it also brought with it a deep loneliness. She moved to the corner where the prayer rugs were kept, kneeling down and closing her eyes. The familiar rhythm of prayer—something she had done since she was a child—should have brought her comfort, but now it only felt like a reminder of everything that was slipping through her fingers.

"Ya Allah," she whispered, her voice barely audible. "Why do I still carry this pain? Why do I feel so far from you?"

For a long moment, she sat in silence, the weight of her words pressing down on her chest. She had been so angry with God, so angry for the things that had happened to her. But now, as she knelt there, her heart heavy with the burden of it all, she felt a flicker of something else—something that had been buried deep inside her for so long: forgiveness.

Not for Amir. Not yet. But for herself. The realization hit her like a tidal wave—she had spent so long blaming herself, carrying the weight of the past as though it were her fault. But it wasn't. She hadn't caused the pain. She hadn't chosen to live through the things she had endured. It wasn't her fault.

With that realization came a small, fragile sense of peace. Maybe she didn't have to forgive everything right away. Maybe healing didn't come in grand gestures, but in small, quiet moments of self-compassion.

She stood up, wiping the tears that had begun to fall, and walked out of the mosque, feeling lighter than she had in days. It wasn't much, but it was a start.

That evening, as she sat with her father and Azaan, she felt a shift within herself. There was still so much to face, so much to untangle, but for the first time in a long time, she felt the smallest spark of hope.

Her father looked at her, his eyes filled with a mix of worry and hope. "Are you okay, Zara?" he asked softly.

Zara met his gaze, and for the first time in a long time, she didn't feel the weight of resentment. Instead, she simply nodded.

"I'm getting there," she said quietly. "I think... I think I'm starting to forgive myself."

10

The Fractured Foundation

The silence in the room was suffocating. Zara sat across from her father, the weight of his words yet to settle, his eyes brimming with tears. Her own were dry, locked behind a wall she was too tired to tear down.

"Zara," her father began, his voice filled with sorrow, "I've failed you. I was blind when I should have seen your pain. I wasn't there when you needed me most. I—"

Zara's hand tightened around the edge of the chair, her gaze distant. She wanted to hear him, to believe the remorse in his voice, but she couldn't. Not yet.

"You weren't there, Baba," she cut him off, her voice trembling with a quiet fury. "You weren't there when Faisal took everything from me. You weren't there when I was a child and cried silently in that dark storeroom. You weren't there when his hands were on me, when he told me that it was a secret. You weren't there when my innocence was stolen, and no one, not even you, noticed."

Her breath caught as she felt the familiar sting of old memories, ones she'd spent so many years trying to bury.

"Do you know what it's like to be a child, Baba, and to have your body turned into something vile? Do you know what it's like to scream inside and have no one hear? To wish you could die just to escape the shame of it?" Zara's voice cracked, her eyes burning with the weight of the truth that had never been spoken.

"And when I finally found the courage to speak, when I thought Amir, my closest friend, would be there for me—he wasn't. He looked at me like I was dirty, like I was used." Her hands balled into fists, the raw pain flashing in her eyes. "He turned away from me when I needed him the most. On the day of our nikkah, I told him everything—everything I had hidden for years. I wanted him to see me, to understand. But he couldn't. He couldn't bear the truth, and instead, he left me to rot in my own guilt, my own shame. He abandoned me, Baba. He left me thinking that I was unworthy, that my past made me unclean. He walked away from me, as if I were a broken thing."

Zara's voice lowered, her breath ragged as she let the silence hang heavy between them. She wasn't finished.

"And you? You never believed me, Baba. Not when I was a child, not when I told you what happened. You chose to ignore me, to silence me. You never asked. You never looked." Her eyes filled with bitterness. "I tried to scream for help, and you didn't hear me. Or maybe you just didn't want to. Maybe it was easier to pretend everything was fine."

Her father's face crumbled under her words, tears streaming down his face as he reached out toward her. But Zara pulled back, her body trembling with a mixture of anger and sorrow.

"I can't forgive you, Baba," she whispered, her voice raw. "Not yet. Maybe not ever. But you want to know what I needed from you? To see me. To believe me. Not as a victim, not as someone broken, but as your daughter—someone who deserved your protection, your love, your trust."

Her father's hand dropped to the table, his head hanging low. The guilt in his eyes was suffocating.

Zara stood up abruptly, her heart racing, the emotions a storm inside her. "You failed me," she whispered, almost to herself. "And I've been carrying that weight ever since."

The air between them was thick with unspoken words, and as Zara turned to leave, a single tear fell from her eye. It wasn't forgiveness, not yet. But it was a crack in the wall, the first step toward something new.

11

The Quiet Storm

Zara stood on the balcony, the cool morning air brushing against her skin, but it did little to soothe the tightness in her chest. The city of Srinagar sprawled beneath her, still and quiet, almost as if it, too, were holding its breath. Zara watched the rising sun cast its pale light across the valley, the mountains in the distance wrapped in mist, like a veil hiding the world from view. She had always found solace in this landscape—the way it seemed so constant, untouched by time.

But today, everything felt different. Everything felt fragile.

She could still hear her father's voice, still see the rawness in his eyes, the weight of his guilt. But even as he had apologized, even as he had begged for her forgiveness, Zara knew she wasn't ready to offer it. She wasn't sure if she ever would be. The past hung between them, a chasm too wide to bridge in one moment.

Her thoughts shifted to Amir. Her heart twisted with the memory of him, of the boy she had loved, and of the man who had abandoned her when she had needed him most. The pain of that abandonment was still fresh, still like an open wound that bled with every thought of him.

Why had he left her? Why had he believed she was "used"? The question haunted her, reverberating in her mind, but there was no answer, only silence. He had been her confidant, her protector, and yet when it came time for him to stand by her, he had walked away, as if her past had made her unworthy of his love.

Zara squeezed her eyes shut, trying to push the memories away, but they flooded back, unbidden. Faisal's hands, the darkness of the storeroom, the whispers that promised silence. She had never spoken about that night in detail, not to anyone—not even Amir. But now, she realized, she was speaking about it in fragments, to herself, in the quiet of her mind.

It wasn't just the assault. It was everything that followed. The shame, the guilt, the feeling of being dirty, of being someone no one could love. Amir had confirmed that fear, hadn't he? By walking away, by turning his back on her when all she had wanted was understanding.

Zara let out a shaky breath, staring at the mountains again, as if they held the answers she couldn't find. It was exhausting, this constant battle between wanting to move forward and the pull of the past, the way it reached out to her in the stillness.

"Ammi," she whispered, her voice breaking. "What do I do now?"

There was no answer, just the quiet hum of the morning. But Zara knew she couldn't stay here, stuck in this limbo. She couldn't remain trapped in the pain of her father's failure, or in the ghost of Amir's betrayal.

She needed to start taking steps. Tiny steps. But steps, nonetheless.

Turning away from the view, she walked back into the house, the weight of her thoughts still heavy on her. She didn't have all the answers, but for the first time in a long while, she knew she couldn't keep waiting for others to fix her, or to give her the validation she so desperately sought.

The journey to healing, to reclaiming herself, was hers to make. It wouldn't be easy. But it was time.

Chapter 12: The First Step

Zara stood in front of the mirror, staring at the reflection she barely recognized. The woman who looked back at her was not the same girl who had once trembled in the face of Faisal's cruelty, not the same girl who had been abandoned by Amir. No, this woman was different. She was scarred, yes. But there was something else now. A flicker of something beneath the surface—a glimmer of strength, fragile but undeniable.

For the first time in years, she wasn't looking for approval. She wasn't waiting for someone to save her, to tell her she was enough. Zara reached up and touched her face, tracing the outline of her cheekbone, her jawline. She was learning to see herself through her own eyes, not through the eyes of others.

Her hand hovered near her neck, where the scars of the past lay hidden beneath layers of fabric. She had never been able to wear anything that felt freeing, anything that might let her feel less trapped in her own skin. But today, for the first time, she wasn't ashamed.

Zara picked up the long scarf she had always wrapped tightly around her neck, but this time, she didn't tie it in the usual way. She let it fall loosely around her shoulders, a quiet defiance against the shame that had long consumed her. She was no longer hiding herself from the world.

Taking a deep breath, she turned away from the mirror and walked out of her room. The house was quiet, but a subtle shift was in the air. Zara knew it wasn't just her that was changing—it was her relationship with the world, too. She wasn't the girl she used to be, not the silent, invisible child who had carried her pain alone. She was someone new, and she wasn't going to let that part of her die in the shadow of her past.

Zara stepped outside, the cold air biting at her skin, but it was a relief. She could feel the weight of her past in every step she took, but with each step, it felt a little lighter. The memories were still there, always there, but they were no longer the center of her existence.

She walked toward the small garden in front of the house, where she had spent many hours as a child, hiding from the world. Today, the garden seemed different, as though it too had grown, just as she had. The flowers, once forgotten and neglected, were blooming again. And for the first time in years, Zara saw the beauty in them.

"Ammi," she whispered, looking up at the sky. "I'm trying. I'm trying to be whole again."

Her mother's absence still felt like a hole in her chest, but the more Zara allowed herself to step into the world, the more she felt her mother's presence in the spaces she had once feared. She was learning to breathe without the weight of all her secrets, without the shame that had suffocated her for so long.

There was no grand moment of catharsis, no instant fix. But for the first time, Zara allowed herself to feel something other than pain—something that felt like hope. Maybe it wasn't forgiveness yet, and maybe the road to healing was still long. But it was a road she was willing to walk.

As she stood there, feeling the sun on her face, Zara realized that this was the beginning of something new. She wasn't defined by what had happened to her. She was more than the broken girl who had once hidden in the dark. And for the first time in her life, she felt like she was worthy of a future—one that was her own.

12

The First Step

Zara had avoided the local coffee shop for weeks, but today, something pulled her there. She had no reason to expect anything extraordinary—just the need for space away from the house, away from the weight of her thoughts. A small escape, just for a while.

The barista behind the counter greeted her with a familiar smile. She had come here often in the past, but it had always been in quiet desperation, hiding in the crowd, avoiding eye contact, making sure no one saw her pain. Today, though, Zara felt strangely calm, almost detached from her usual fears. She wasn't trying to disappear into the background anymore.

She ordered a chai, and as she waited for it to be made, she found herself standing by the window, gazing out at the busy street. The world seemed so far away—so full of noise and movement, like a place she no longer truly belonged. And yet, here she was, standing still in the middle of it.

She wasn't sure how long she had been standing there when a soft voice interrupted her thoughts.

"Zara?"

She turned slowly, her heart skipping a beat. There, standing just a few feet away, was Leyla. Zara hadn't seen her in years, but the familiarity of her presence made something in Zara shift—an unexpected warmth that both surprised and comforted her.

Leyla had been a friend from her childhood, someone Zara had once trusted without question. They had spent hours together as young girls, sharing secrets, dreaming of the future. But time, and the weight of Zara's secrets, had pulled them apart. They hadn't spoken since Zara's world had fallen apart, since her trauma had taken over and she had retreated into herself.

"Leyla..." Zara said, her voice uncertain. "It's... it's been a long time."

Leyla's eyes softened. She stepped closer, her expression a mix of concern and something else—something that felt almost like understanding, like she had known all along the pain Zara had carried.

"I saw you sitting here," Leyla said, her voice quiet. "I thought maybe you could use a friend."

Zara didn't know how to respond. She had never shared her story with Leyla, never let anyone close enough to see the broken parts of her. But there was something in Leyla's gaze—something unspoken—that made Zara hesitate. She felt safe in a way she hadn't allowed herself to feel in a long time.

"I..." Zara hesitated. She opened her mouth to speak, to say something light, something to deflect, but the words caught in her throat. For the first time in a while, she realized she didn't have to hide. Leyla wasn't asking for answers; she was offering something else entirely—companionship, understanding, a simple connection.

"Can we sit down?" Zara finally asked, her voice tentative but genuine.

Leyla smiled and nodded, and the two of them took a seat at a small table by the window. The world continued to move outside, but inside the coffee shop, it felt like a pause—a small moment of peace in the chaos.

For the next few minutes, they talked about nothing important—the kind of conversation that was so familiar, it almost felt like nothing had changed. Zara found herself laughing softly at Leyla's jokes, feeling a warmth spread through her chest that had been absent for too long.

But then, as the silence between them grew, Leyla looked at Zara with a softness that made her heart ache.

"You know," Leyla said, her voice gentle, "if you ever want to talk... about anything, I'm here. I don't know what happened, Zara, but I can see it. I can see that something's different about you now."

Zara's chest tightened, her breath catching in her throat. She had been so used to hiding her truth, so accustomed to the silence that surrounded her trauma. But here, in this small, quiet space, something shifted.

"I..." Zara began, but the words stalled. What could she say? How could she explain the years of pain, the suffering, the weight of the secret that had shaped her life?

But Leyla reached across the table, her hand hovering just over Zara's. "You don't have to say anything," she whispered. "But I'm here, if you ever want to."

Zara felt the weight of her words settle into her chest, the truth of what Leyla was offering. She wasn't being asked to share everything at once, to bare her soul in a single moment. She was being given the space to be real, to simply exist as she was, without judgment.

For the first time in a long while, Zara felt a crack in the walls she had built around herself. Maybe it wouldn't be today, maybe it wouldn't be tomorrow, but one day, she knew she might be ready to share her story with someone who didn't turn away, someone who might listen.

For now, though, this moment, this quiet connection, was enough.

13

The Quiet Cnnection

Zara had avoided the local coffee shop for weeks, but today, something pulled her there. She had no reason to expect anything extraordinary—just the need for space away from the house, away from the weight of her thoughts. A small escape, just for a while.

The barista behind the counter greeted her with a familiar smile. She had come here often in the past, but it had always been in quiet desperation, hiding in the crowd, avoiding eye contact, making sure no one saw her pain. Today, though, Zara felt strangely calm, almost detached from her usual fears. She wasn't trying to disappear into the background anymore.

She ordered a chai, and as she waited for it to be made, she found herself standing by the window, gazing out at the busy street. The world seemed so far away—so full of noise and movement, like a place she no longer truly belonged. And yet, here she was, standing still in the middle of it.

She wasn't sure how long she had been standing there when a soft voice interrupted her thoughts.

"Zara?"

She turned slowly, her heart skipping a beat. There, standing just a few feet away, was Leyla. Zara hadn't seen her in years, but the familiarity of her presence made something in Zara shift—an unexpected warmth that both surprised and comforted her.

Leyla had been a friend from her childhood, someone Zara had once trusted without question. They had spent hours together as young girls, sharing secrets, dreaming of the future. But time, and the weight of Zara's secrets, had pulled them apart. They hadn't spoken since Zara's world had fallen apart, since her trauma had taken over and she had retreated into herself.

"Leyla..." Zara said, her voice uncertain. "It's... it's been a long time."

Leyla's eyes softened. She stepped closer, her expression a mix of concern and something else—something that felt almost like understanding, like she had known all along the pain Zara had carried.

"I saw you sitting here," Leyla said, her voice quiet. "I thought maybe you could use a friend."

Zara didn't know how to respond. She had never shared her story with Leyla, never let anyone close enough to see the broken parts of her. But there was something in Leyla's gaze—something unspoken—that made Zara hesitate. She felt safe in a way she hadn't allowed herself to feel in a long time.

"I..." Zara hesitated. She opened her mouth to speak, to say something light, something to deflect, but the words caught in her throat. For the first time in a while, she realized she didn't have to hide. Leyla wasn't asking for answers; she was offering something else entirely—companionship, understanding, a simple connection.

"Can we sit down?" Zara finally asked, her voice tentative but genuine.

Leyla smiled and nodded, and the two of them took a seat at a small table by the window. The world continued to move outside, but inside the coffee shop, it felt like a pause—a small moment of peace in the chaos.

For the next few minutes, they talked about nothing important—the kind of conversation that was so familiar, it almost felt like nothing had changed. Zara found herself laughing softly at Leyla's jokes, feeling a warmth spread through her chest that had been absent for too long.

But then, as the silence between them grew, Leyla looked at Zara with a softness that made her heart ache.

"You know," Leyla said, her voice gentle, "if you ever want to talk... about anything, I'm here. I don't know what happened, Zara, but I can see it. I can see that something's different about you now."

Zara's chest tightened, her breath catching in her throat. She had been so used to hiding her truth, so accustomed to the silence that surrounded her trauma. But here, in this small, quiet space, something shifted.

"I..." Zara began, but the words stalled. What could she say? How could she explain the years of pain, the suffering, the weight of the secret that had shaped her life?

But Leyla reached across the table, her hand hovering just over Zara's. "You don't have to say anything," she whispered. "But I'm here, if you ever want to."

Zara felt the weight of her words settle into her chest, the truth of what Leyla was offering. She wasn't being asked to share everything at once, to bare her soul in a single moment. She was being given the space to be real, to simply exist as she was, without judgment.

For the first time in a long while, Zara felt a crack in the walls she had built around herself. Maybe it wouldn't be today, maybe it wouldn't be tomorrow, but one day, she knew she might be ready to share her story with someone who didn't turn away, someone who might listen.

For now, though, this moment, this quiet connection, was enough.

14

The Unspoken Truth

Zara found herself standing at the edge of the old, dilapidated building, where her childhood memories had once taken root. The sun had dipped low in the sky, casting a warm orange hue over the abandoned structure. Her heart pounded in the chest, the rhythm of it echoing in her ears as she stood frozen in place.

The building, now a ghost of what it had once been, had always help a strange power over her. It was her that Faisal had violated her, here that the walls had absorbed the screams, here where she had learn't that safety was an illusion. It had always been a place of fear, a place she couldn't even bring herself to look at for years.

But today... today was different.

Leyla had encouraged her to face it, to go back to the places where past still clung to her like a shadow. At first, Zara had resisted. The idea of stepping foot inside the place where it all began seemed impossible, as though it might break her all over again. But there was something else inside her now—a desire to reclaim what had been stolen, to find closure, even if it meant confronting the darkest parts of herself.

With a steadying breath, Zara took a cautious step forward, her boots crunching against the gravel. The familiar scent of dust and decay hit her like a wave. She hesitated, a wave of panic rising in her chest, but she forced herself to keep moving. The door creaked as she pushed it open, its hinges protesting the disturbance.

Inside, the space was as she remembered, dim and musty with shadows clinging to every corner. The broken window just let enough light to illuminate the wreckage of her past. It was a place frozen in time, a place that had witnessed her pain but also the bringing of her strength. She had always seen it as a symbol of everything that had broken her. But now, as she stood inside, she could feel something different, a shift in the air.

Zara closed her eyes for a moment, letting the memories flood over her. She could still hear Faisal's voice, low and cruel, the sensation of his hands over her skin, the feeling of her body betraying her. It was all there, sharp and vivid, but it no longer consumed her. She could remember it now without losing herself in it.

The sound of footsteps from behind startled her, and she turned quickly, her heart racing. But it was only Leyla, who had followed her inside quietly, giving Zara the space she needed.

"I'm here," Leyla said softly, her voice grounding Zara back to the present, "Whenever you're ready."

Zara swallowed, her throat, dry. She hadn't expected the courage to come this quickly. She hadn't expected to feel anything other than fear. But the truth was that she had already carried the weight of this place for so long. What was left to fear?

"I'm ready," Zara whispered, more to herself than to Leyla. She wasn't ready to let the past define her anymore.

She took a slow, deliberate step forward, her eyes scanning the room.

It was still a place of hurt, but Zara could see the cracks in the walls, the small spaces where light was filtering through. She had lived in the dark for so long, but now, she could see the possibility of something new.

Leyla stepped beside her, her hand resting gently on Zara's shoulder, a silent reassurance. Zara didn't flinch, didn't pull away. She simply stood there ,breathing in the air that had once chocked her, and felt a sense of peace that was foreign yet undeniable.

"Thank you," Zara said quietly, her voice, cheeky, but full of resolve. It was first time that she had really faced this place, truly faced what it had represented, and it felt like a small victory. She wasn't running anymore. She wasn't hiding. She was standing in the face of it, and it was no longer her enemy.

Leyla nodded, her expressions soft, and understanding. She didn't need to say anything else. She knew.

Zara took last look around the room, her heart no longer heavy, but lighter— like she had left a piece of herself here and taken something new with her. The past no longer held the same power over her. She would never forget it, but it wouldn't control her anymore.

As they walked out of the building together, the sun was beginning to set, the sky with the shades of pink and gold. Zara felt something shift inside her—a quite strength , a soft rebirth. Was no longer defined by what had happened to her. She was something more now. Something whole.

And for the first time in the long time, Zara felt like that she could breathe again.

15

The Unspoken Bond

Zara woke up early, as she often did, before the rest of the house stirred. The silence of the early morning felt like a familiar companion. She sat at the edge of her bed, her fingers brushing over the fabric of the quilt her mother had once made. Her mother's presence, though gone, still lingered in the small, intimate spaces of her life.

It had been weeks since their conversation—weeks since her father had finally, truly seen her. But even now, the distance between them remained, a quiet undercurrent that neither of them had dared to address. Zara couldn't forget the rawness in his voice when he apologized, the shame that had wracked his body when he had admitted his failure as a father. But she also knew that it wasn't enough. Words could never undo the years of silence and neglect.

She pulled herself from bed and walked into the kitchen. The soft hum of the morning light made everything seem peaceful, almost too peaceful. Her father was already sitting at the table, a cup of tea in front of him. He didn't look up as she entered, but she could feel his eyes on her, waiting. The weight of his gaze felt both familiar and foreign.

Zara hesitated, unsure of what to say or how to bridge the gap between them. The things she had shared with him were still too raw, too new. But she knew something had shifted inside her. She had given him the truth—her truth—and it had been enough to shake the foundation of their relationship. The walls she had built around her heart were crumbling, and she didn't know if she was ready to let him inside completely.

"Morning, Baba," Zara said softly, taking a seat across from him. Her voice was steady, but her heart was racing.

He nodded, offering a small smile, but there was a sadness in his eyes that hadn't been there before. His shoulders were slumped, the weight of guilt still pressing down on him. Zara wanted to reach out, wanted to tell him that she understood, that she had forgiven him in her own way. But she wasn't sure if she could say those words just yet. Forgiveness, for her, was still a process.

"You've been quiet lately," her father said, his voice low. "Are you... are you okay?"

Zara looked at him, really looked at him. There was a vulnerability in his eyes now, something that hadn't been there when she was younger, when she had desperately needed him to see her. The man sitting across from her now was not the same man who had failed to protect her. He had changed—whether for the better, she didn't know yet. But there was something in his face that made her pause, something that made her want to try.

"I'm trying," Zara said quietly, her fingers tracing the rim of her cup. "It's not easy. But I'm trying."

He didn't speak right away, letting the words settle between them. After a moment, he finally spoke, his voice trembling. "Zara... I know I can never take back what happened. But I want you to know that I will do whatever it takes to be there for you now. To make it right."

Zara's chest tightened at his words. They were the ones she had always longed to hear, the words that had eluded her for so long. But now, in the quiet morning light, they felt... incomplete. Words were a start, but Zara needed more than just promises. She needed actions. She needed time to rebuild what had been broken.

"I know, Baba," Zara replied, her voice soft but firm. "But it's not just about saying the right things. It's about showing up. It's about being there, even when it's hard."

Her father's eyes softened, and he nodded. "I understand. And I will. I will try my best."

Zara studied him for a long moment. The silence that passed between them wasn't uncomfortable—it was filled with something else. It was the space where healing could begin.

In that moment, something shifted between them—an unspoken understanding that they both had a long road ahead. Zara wasn't ready to forgive him completely, but she was willing to let him try. She was willing to let him be present in her life again, but it would take time. It would take more than just words—it would take the quiet, steady actions of someone who was truly trying to make amends.

As she stood up from the table, her father reached out, his hand hovering in the air as if unsure whether to touch her. Zara didn't hesitate. She placed her hand gently in his, a simple gesture, but one that carried a weight of its own. It wasn't forgiveness—not yet. But it was the beginning of something.

"Thank you," he whispered, his voice thick with emotion.

Zara didn't respond with words. She simply squeezed his hand, and for the first time in a long while, she allowed herself to feel the faintest glimmer of hope.

16

Echoes of Strength

The days blurred together, each one a quiet repetition of the last. Zara woke up early, like she always did, but now it felt different. There was a sense of anticipation in the air, something unspoken that hung over her like a cloud, heavy and yet hopeful.

She had spent most of her life trying to avoid things—avoiding the past, avoiding confrontation, avoiding the pain that came with facing her truth. But lately, something inside her had shifted. She wasn't sure when it had happened, but she knew it had. Her steps, though still hesitant, were now more deliberate. She was no longer moving in circles, but forward, even if the path was unclear.

One evening, as the sky outside turned a dusky pink, Zara sat by the window of her bedroom, watching the world go by. Her fingers traced the old photographs that lined the walls—moments from before everything had fallen apart. Before the weight of the world had pressed down on her, before Faisal's betrayal, before Amir's abandonment.

Her hand lingered on a picture of her mother, standing in the garden with her hands raised, smiling at the camera. Zara had never fully understood the calm strength in her mother's smile until now. It was as if her mother had known what the world was capable of, had known what Zara would face, and yet she had still stood tall. Zara thought of her mother often now, as though the very air around her had become a conduit for her mother's guidance.

The knock on the door interrupted her thoughts.

"Zara?" her father's voice came from the other side, hesitant and soft, as if he too felt the weight of the unspoken things between them. "I need to talk to you."

Zara stood, setting the photograph back in its place before walking to the door. When she opened it, her father was standing there, looking smaller than she remembered. There was no anger in his face now, no defensiveness. Just the quiet acceptance of someone who had begun to understand the depth of their mistakes.

"Come in," Zara said, stepping aside.

He entered and sat down at the edge of her bed, his hands clasped in front of him. There was something fragile in the air, a heaviness that neither of them was ready to ignore, but neither wanted to confront directly.

"I've been thinking," her father began, his voice steady, but the lines of worry etched on his face were visible. "I want to help you more. Not just with words, but with actions. I want to be here for you. I want you to know I'm willing to do whatever it takes."

Zara watched him for a long moment, taking in his words, weighing them against the past. She had spent so many years wanting him to say those things, hoping he would see her pain, hoping he would finally believe her.

And now, here he was, offering it. But something inside her still hesitated. She wasn't ready to give him everything—not yet.

"You've already done something," Zara said softly, sitting down next to him. "By finally acknowledging what happened. By not pretending everything was fine. But actions take time. And I need time, too."

Her father nodded slowly, his eyes reflecting the same understanding. "I know. And I will wait. But I'm here, Zara. Whenever you're ready."

Zara turned her gaze to the window, her fingers tracing the edge of the curtain. The words were familiar, but for the first time, they didn't feel like empty promises. Her father's presence, though quiet, was a steady comfort. He hadn't been able to protect her in the past, but in this moment, he was doing what he could.

"I'm not ready to forgive you yet, Baba," Zara said, her voice barely above a whisper, "but I'm willing to try."

And that was enough.

Her father didn't respond. He didn't have to. His silent presence, his willingness to wait, spoke louder than any words could.

After a few moments of comfortable silence, Zara stood up and moved toward the small bookshelf in the corner of her room. She had been thinking about this for days, but the time felt right. She pulled down the small journal her mother had kept, the one that had been left behind when she passed. It was filled with pages of thoughts, poems, dreams—words that had never been shared aloud.

Zara opened it to a page near the end and began to read. Her mother's handwriting was delicate, beautiful, but what caught Zara's eye were the words written in the margin: "You are stronger than you know. Don't forget that."

She read it again, feeling the weight of her mother's presence in the room, as though the words had been meant for her all along. She glanced at her father, who had been watching her quietly, and for the first time, she saw something else in his eyes—a recognition that mirrored her own.

She wasn't sure where this road would lead, or how much healing was still left to be done. But in that moment, as the last rays of sunlight filtered through the window, Zara felt something settle in her chest: peace. It wasn't the kind of peace that came from having everything figured out. It was a peace that came from knowing she was no longer carrying the burden alone. It was the quiet strength of knowing she was capable of something far greater than she had ever given herself credit for.

"I think I'm ready to move forward," Zara said, her voice clear and firm. "But it's going to take time. For both of us."

Her father nodded, a faint smile tugging at the corners of his lips. "I'll be here," he said quietly. "Every step of the way."

17

The Strength To Begin Again

Zara's footsteps echoed softly in the empty hallway as she made her way to the small room at the back of the house, where she used to paint. It had been years since she had picked up a brush. Years since the colors had come to life beneath her fingers, since the canvas had been a space for her to breathe.

But today felt different. Today, there was a quiet pull inside her, urging her to return to something that had once brought her peace, something that hadn't been tainted by the darkness of the past.

The door creaked as she pushed it open, revealing the room she had abandoned so many years ago. Dust had settled over the furniture, the faint smell of old paint lingering in the air. The easel stood untouched in the corner, a blank canvas waiting for her.

Zara stood in the doorway for a moment, her heart racing as she took in the space that had once been her refuge. The room was filled with memories—of afternoons spent lost in color, of a time before the world had become so heavy. It felt like coming home, and yet, it also felt strange. The act of picking up a brush again was more than just a return to an old hobby. It was a step toward something more, something that had been buried deep inside her for so long.

Slowly, she walked toward the easel, her fingers grazing the old brushes that lay scattered across the table. She picked one up, the bristles worn and familiar, and dipped it into the paint. The first stroke felt hesitant, unsure, but as the color spread across the canvas, something inside her shifted.

It wasn't the masterpiece she had once dreamed of, but that wasn't the point. The point was that she was here, standing in this space, allowing herself to feel something other than pain. For the first time in what felt like forever, Zara allowed herself to be vulnerable—to create something without fear of judgment or failure.

The hours slipped by unnoticed as Zara painted. The strokes of color blurred together, the canvas coming to life in front of her. She didn't know exactly what she was painting, but it didn't matter. What mattered was that she was finally letting go—letting go of the silence, the shame, the weight of everything she had carried for so long.

As the final stroke was added to the canvas, Zara stepped back and looked at what she had created. It was an abstract piece—wild and free, filled with bursts of color that seemed to pulse with energy. It was messy, imperfect, but it was hers. It was her soul laid bare, stripped of all the barriers she had built over the years.

Tears welled up in her eyes as she stood there, staring at the painting. She didn't know if it was the act of creating or the release of emotions she had locked away for so long, but in that moment, she felt something she hadn't in years:

hope.

There was still so much work to be done. So much healing left. But for the first time, Zara felt like she was on the right path. She was no longer running from the past, no longer hiding from the things that had shaped her. She was learning to stand tall in the face of it, to accept herself and her story without shame.

She left the room quietly, her heart lighter than it had been in a long time. As she passed by the mirror in the hallway, she caught a glimpse of herself. Zara looked at the reflection for a long moment, her eyes searching her own face. She saw the scars, both visible and invisible, but she also saw something else. She saw strength. The strength to begin again.

18

The Silent Strength

Zara stood on the balcony, the cool air of the evening brushing against her skin. The city below, once a chaotic swirl of memories, now felt distant, as though it were no longer part of the world she inhabited. The weight of her past was still there, pressing gently against her chest, but it no longer consumed her. She had come to understand that her story wasn't one of tragedy—it was one of survival. And that survival had brought her here, to this moment.

Her father had apologized, and she had let him in. She had reclaimed pieces of herself—through art, through forgiveness, through the quiet moments of reflection. But the most important step was the one she had taken on her own: the decision to live again, to walk forward without carrying the burden of shame that had defined her for so long.

Zara's fingers tightened around the railing as her thoughts turned inward, as they often did when she allowed herself to be still. She thought of her mother, of the lessons passed down in whispered words and dreams. She thought of the girls and women she had never met, the ones who suffered in silence, just like she had.

For years, Zara had believed that she was broken. That her pain, her story, made her unworthy of love, of peace, of a future. But now, she understood that her pain was not the end of her. It was a part of her, yes, but it didn't define her. She had the power to shape her own narrative. She had done it, one step at a time, and that was something worth celebrating.

Zara closed her eyes, breathing in deeply. She thought of all the times she had wanted to scream, wanted to be heard, but had stayed silent instead. Now, she knew what it meant to give a voice to that silence. It was no longer about waiting for someone to listen—it was about speaking, even when no one asked her to. It was about owning her story, her truth, and sharing it with the world.

She had learned that healing wasn't a destination—it was a journey. One that she would continue on, every day, in small moments, in quiet victories. She had come a long way, but there was still more to do. There would be days when the weight of it all would threaten to pull her under again, and on those days, she would remember the strength it had taken to get this far. And she would keep going.

Her phone buzzed on the table behind her, pulling her from her thoughts. Zara turned and walked back inside, her steps firm and deliberate. The screen lit up with a message from an unknown number. She hesitated for only a moment before opening it.

"Zara, I heard your story. I'm sorry for what happened to you. But I want you to know you're not alone. I believe you."

Zara read the words twice, her heart suddenly heavy with a mixture of gratitude and sorrow. She didn't know who this person was, but she knew they understood. And that understanding was enough. It was a reminder that she was no longer isolated, no longer a prisoner of her silence.

She typed a quick reply, her fingers steady.

"Thank you. I'm learning to live again. I'm learning to heal."

Zara set the phone down and turned back to the balcony, the city now a soft blur beneath the fading light. She wasn't sure what the future held, but for the first time in years, she felt ready to face it. Her past would always be a part of her, but it no longer held the power to control her. She was ready to live—for herself, for the women who had been silenced, and for those who still needed to find their voice.

And as the stars began to fill the sky, Zara took a deep breath and smiled. It wasn't a perfect smile, but it was real. It was the smile of someone who had learned that strength wasn't in being unbreakable. It was in breaking and still choosing to stand, to fight, to live.

Epilogue-"to Those Who Carry Silence

The unknown narrator speaks:

"There are women who carry their silence like stones in their chest, believing the weight is theirs alone to bear. But silence does not make pain less real. It does not make truth less true. And it does not make them any less whole."

"Zara was one of them. And maybe, so are you."

"But listen—there will come a day when the weight feels lighter, when the past no longer holds your voice hostage. It will not be sudden. It will not be easy. But it will happen."

"And when it does, you will know—"

"You were never meant to drown. You were meant to rise."

www.ingramcontent.com/pod-product-compliance
Lightning Source LLC
La Vergne TN
LVHW041132150826
845673LV00007B/2290

* 9 7 9 8 8 9 7 2 4 0 8 7 6 *